I'm Kayla and this is my dog, Kugel. Tonight, our family is having a very exciting meal. It's called a seder.

Kayla and Kugel's Almost-Perfect Passover

By Ann D. Koffsky

This **PJ BOOK** belongs to

_____

_____

PJ Library
JEWISH BEDTIME STORIES and SONGS

APPLES & HONEY PRESS

With thanks to Lynn and Ed Koffsky for raising
a good husband for me, and for all their
continued love and support.
—ADK

Apples & Honey Press
An imprint of Behrman House
Behrman House, 11 Edison Place, Springfield, New Jersey 07081

www.applesandhoneypress.com

ISBN 978-1-68115-508-1

Library of Congress Control Number: 2015023229

Design by Elynn Cohen
Edited by Dena Neusner
Printed in China
1 3 5 7 9 8 6 4 2

031822.4K1/B1180/A2

First we have to get ready. I'm
making a cover for my haggadah,
and Kugel's helping.

Oh no!

Kugel found the glue.

Then we begin
the seder.

There are
special
foods to
eat and
drink.

Kugel, watch out for
that grape juice!

I like dipping the
curly parsley
into salt water.

Kugel loves
munching the
matzah . . .
and making a
crumbly mess.

Kugel, let's sing the
Four Questions together.

I tell Kugel about how my great-, great-, great-, great-, great- (lots of greats) grandparents were slaves to the mean and terrible Pharaoh in Egypt.

After some
amazing miracles,
they became free.

Foods have meaning at the seder. Freedom is sweet.

Yum!

Sweet charoset.

After a delicious dinner comes the part of the seder I like best—finding the afikoman.

Oh no, Kugel. Bring that back!

KUGEL!!!

Kugel, we can't continue our seder without the afikoman. Where is it?

Good boy, Kugel.

Now the seder is complete.
We asked the questions,
told the story, and ate
the foods.

What's wrong, Kugel? What are we missing?

Songs! We always finish
our seder with songs.
Let's celebrate and sing!

Happy
Passover!

Can you find these things at Kayla and Kugel's seder?

SEDER PLATE

holds the seder foods

חרוסת

מרור

AFIKOMAN

a piece of matzah
that we hide

ELIJAH'S CUP

holds grape juice
or wine

מרור

HAGGADAH

a book that helps
everyone enjoy the
seder together

The Story of Passover

The first Passover happened long ago in the far-away country of Egypt. A mean and powerful king, called Pharaoh, ruled Egypt. Worried that the Jewish people would one day fight against him, Pharaoh decided that these people must become his slaves. As slaves, the Jewish people worked very hard. Every day, from morning until night, they hammered, dug, and carried heavy bricks. They built palaces and cities and worked without rest. The Jewish people hated being slaves. They cried and asked God for help. God chose a man named Moses to lead the Jewish people. Moses went to Pharaoh and said, "God is not happy with the way you treat the Jewish people. He wants you to let the Jewish people leave Egypt and go into the desert, where they will be free." But Pharaoh stamped his foot and shouted, "No, I will never let the Jewish people go!" Moses warned, "If you do not listen to God, many terrible things, called plagues, will come to your land." But Pharaoh would not listen, and so the plagues arrived. First, the water turned to blood. Next, frogs and, later, wild animals ran in and out of homes. Balls of hail fell from the sky and bugs, called locusts, ate all of the Egyptians' food.

Each time a new plague began, Pharaoh would cry, "Moses, I'll let the Jewish people go. Just stop this horrible plague!" Yet no sooner would God take away the plague than Pharaoh would shout: "No, I've changed my mind. The Jews must stay!" So God sent more plagues. Finally, as the tenth plague arrived, Pharaoh ordered the Jews to leave Egypt.

Fearful that Pharaoh might again change his mind, the Jewish people packed quickly. They had no time to prepare food and no time to allow their dough to rise into puffy bread. They had only enough time to make a flat, cracker-like bread called matzah. They hastily tied the matzah to their backs and ran from their homes.

The people had not travelled far before Pharaoh commanded his army to chase after them and bring them back to Egypt. The Jews dashed forward, but stopped when they reached a large sea. The sea was too big to swim across. Frightened that Pharaoh's men would soon reach them, the people prayed to God, and a miracle occurred. The sea opened up. Two walls of water stood in front of them and a dry, sandy path stretched between the walls. The Jews ran across. Just as they reached the other side, the walls of water fell and the path disappeared. The sea now separated the Jews from the land of Egypt. They were free!

Each year at Passover, we eat special foods, sing songs, tell stories, and participate in a seder – a special meal designed to help us remember this miraculous journey from slavery to freedom.